Rubin and the lost horse of

A story with illustrations, magic and riddles

by

Sam Preece

Eastrop Cottage Publishing

First published in Great Britain in 2018 by

Eastrop Cottage Publishing

Up Nately, Hants. RG27 9PS

A CIP catalogue record of this book is available from the British Library.

ISBN 978-1-5272-2046-1

Eastrop Cottage Publishing

is an imprint of

Dolman Scott Ltd

www.dolmanscott.co.uk

For my six very special grandchildren

Cameron & Molly,

Owen & Zara,

Austin & Verity.

Much Love from Grandpa Sam

List of illustrations

Rubin and the lost horse of Merrithorpe

Chapter I

The crone

Once, long ago, when mankind travelled mainly on foot or on horseback, a poor and lonely youth wandered daily through the countryside in search of food and a dry place to rest his head for the night.

He had nearly forgotten better times since becoming an orphan. His only possessions were a flint and dry material, which he kept in a ragged pocket. With these, he was able to light a fire for warmth or to cook a rabbit, if he had been lucky enough to catch one. Generally, he was able to survive by foraging[1] in hedgerows for seasonable[2] nuts and berries.

The young lad's name was Rubin.

One day, whilst wandering in search of food, he was distracted by a disturbance in a nearby thicket. The loudness of the noises, a thundering sound and cracking of branches, alarmed him and upon looking up from the ground he was confronted by a run-away horse with long flowing mane and feathered fetlocks[3]. Not just any horse, but the most beautiful creature of its kind that Rubin had ever seen. It was an odd-coloured horse, one with patches of black, brown and white, neither skewbald[4] nor piebald.[5]

It was soon aware of Rubin and as he approached, the horse halted and on the very spot where it had stopped, it pawed the ground, first with its left leg, then its right. Then it hesitated before making several pirouettes[6] as if trying to converse in some way.

Suddenly, with great speed, it disappeared into the wood on the other side of the path.

As he watched the horse gallop away, he noticed something glinting in the sunlight. Searching for a while on all fours, he took from the spot a shiny gold horseshoe.

"I wish---I," Rubin said aloud to himself, which in his loneliness was not unusual.

A dark shadow, which at first he thought was his own, remained on the ground as he moved and then he realised someone was stood behind him.

A dark shadow, which at first he thought was his own, remained on the ground as he moved and then he realised someone was stood behind him.
Looking round, he saw that an old crone[7] was leaning over him, partly supporting her weight on a gnarled and twisted walking stick.
Unlike the horse, she had appeared quite noiselessly.

"What were you about to say dearie?" said the crone.

"I---I wish I could own the horse that ran out of the wood, for it is the most beautiful animal I have ever seen and it pranced before me as if trying to convey some message, or riddle maybe," replied Rubin.

"Firstly," said the crone, "you should always use wishes sparingly, most people are allowed only three in their lives."

She continued, "That horse which you yearn to possess is almost certainly one which belongs to The Grand Duke of Merrithorpe. I know of this, because I am the wise woman of the wood, some call me a witch, I have a sixth sense and see everything which happens in the forest, beyond the gates of the castle."

"When out hunting only a few days ago," said the crone, "the Grand Duke spotted the mare and being a man of great taste, he was so impressed by her beauty that he bought her from the travelling horse-coper[8] who was leading her."

Then the crone told Rubin how the horse-coper had advised the Grand Duke that it was important to know the horse's name, because the mare would only stay with someone who could discover it. The horse-coper had also explained to the Duke that he did not know her name and so he found it difficult to keep her to himself.

The crone also told Rubin how the Grand Duke thought it would be easy to guess the name but the mare did not react to any that he had tried. In fact he only seemed to annoy her.

"This morning," said the crone, "the lock on her stable door had been forced and she had obviously been stolen, but since you have just seen her alone, she must have escaped her captor. The Duke is very upset at losing her and has sent all of his servants and estate workers to search for her."

“I am trying to help,” continued the crone, “but I doubt if I will ever catch up with her because I am feeble, my legs are old and the joints worn and they can scarcely carry me.”

“I too will look for that beautiful horse in my wanderings,” said Rubin and if I find her, I will return her to the Grand Duke, her rightful owner.”

“That is very kind of you dearie,” said the crone, “and that makes me certain that you will deserve all the good luck that horseshoe will surely bring you.”

“Thank you,” said Rubin, as he tucked the horseshoe safely inside his shirt.

With that, they each went their own way.

After he wandered back into the wood, Rubin saw several signs of where the horse had been. Broken branches and flattened grass led Rubin back to a tree where he had previously found several apples, but now there were only two apples lying beneath it.

What he did find though, was another golden horseshoe, which he picked up together with the remaining apples.
He began to eat one apple and put the other into his ragged pocket, thinking he might use it to tempt the horse close enough to catch her, if he should be lucky enough to see her again.

Rubin hid the second horseshoe inside his oversized and ragged shirt, separating it from the first with sufficient dry grass to prevent them from clanking together.
As Rubin was quite a thin boy you would not have noticed that he had hidden anything there.

Each of the two horseshoes Rubin had found, had marks cut in their edges. One had three and the other two. Rubin assumed these were farrier’s marks indicating which hoof they had to be fitted to.

Meanings of some words in chapter one

[1]Foraging ---- *search widely for food.*

[2]Seasonable ---- *to be found at certain times of the year.*

[3]Fetlock ---- *the large leg joint immediately above a horses hoof.*

[4]Skewbald ---- *a horse with coloured patches of brown and white. **

[5]Piebald ---- *a horse with black and white patches like the magpie. **

**The army who favoured horses of regular colour and form rejected these horses but their strength and beauty made them much valued by other horse lovers and they were particularly the horse of choice for the gypsy folk.*

[6]Pirouette ---- *spinning around like a ballet dancer.*

[7]Crone ---- *an ugly old woman.*

[8]Horse-coper ---- *a horse dealer.*

When he came to a toyshop, he was <u>not</u> immediately intrigued, as you or I would have been, by the variety of wooden toys on display, but his eyes became glued to a man sitting on a plank above the shop doorway.

Chapter II

The signwriter

Several weeks had passed and Rubin's wanderings had brought him to a small village and although he was still hoping to catch up with the horse, the sights and sounds there had for the time being, distracted him.
From some distance away, the first thing he saw was a golden cockerel glinting in the sunlight on top of the church spire. This was only the third golden thing he had ever seen in his life and he thought it just as fascinating as the two golden horseshoes, which he still carried tucked inside his ragged shirt.

He soon came to a row of village shops - a butcher, baker, and yes, even a candlestick maker - there was also a grocer, a sweet shop and more,

He had never seen such sights or smelled such wonderful smells before.

When he came to a toyshop, he was not immediately intrigued, as you or I would have been, by the variety of wooden toys on display, but his eyes became glued to a man sitting on a plank above the shop doorway.

The man was a signwriter and he was renewing the lettering and painting shadows around the letters so that they stood out as though they were hanging in space.

"I wish---I."

Once again, Rubin was unable to keep his thoughts to himself.

"What did you say?" asked the signwriter from the plank above.

"I wish I could do what you're doing," blurted Rubin.

"I wish you could, too," said the signwriter. "For I have so much painting and signwriting to get done in this and several other villages and it must all be done while the weather holds.

After that I have to paint hundreds of toys to sell in this shop before Christmas."

Although the signwriter was a kindly man, he soon realised that Rubin did not look like the sort of boy that had received much education.

"Can you read and write?" he asked.

Rubin just looked puzzled.

"You would need to know your alphabet to work with me," said the signwriter.

"What is an alphabet?" asked Rubin.

"It's all the letters," said the signwriter. "You have to know all your letters to be a signwriter and then there're the numbers - they're not so difficult to learn as there are only ten of them, like the fingers and thumbs on your two hands."

"Then," he went on, "you must know a little math-er-magics so that you can measure and set the letters and numbers out neatly."

"Would you be able to teach me, sir?" said Rubin.

"I like your spirit, young'un, but to teach you all that would take up too much of my time," replied the signwriter.

He continued, "What you need to do is to go to the wise woman of the village, she runs the Dame school." He thought for a moment then added, "I have to see her soon about some of the school paintwork which gets regularly damaged by the school children, if I ask, perhaps she would agree to take you on as a pupil for a while."

Clearly Rubin would not be able to pay the school fees, but the signwriter was hatching a little plan, which could be not only to his own advantage, but to the advantages of both Rubin and the dame as well.

"Have you ever done any painting, young'un?" he asked

"No, sir," said Rubin. "Well, I am certainly happy to teach you to do some straightforward painting," said the signwriter. "I have a little more work to do on this shop sign, so why don't you meet me here again tomorrow?"

The next morning, Rubin was the first to show up at the toyshop because he hadn't really left it, he had simply settled down for the night in the shop doorway after the signwriter had cleaned and packed away his brushes and had set off for his home.

Luckily, the shopkeeper and his wife lived above the shop and had no idea that they had an uninvited guest sleeping in the doorway below. However when they came downstairs next morning, they noticed his face, pressed against the shop window. This did not cause them concern as they often saw other children gazing longingly at the toys.

One very special toy had attracted Rubin's attention. It was a large rocking horse painted black, brown and white with a long flowing mane made of hemp, tacked neatly to the back of its neck.

"Hello, young'un," said the signwriter as he came up to Rubin. "Do you like my painted rocking horse?"

"Yes, it's lovely, did you make it?" Rubin asked.

"The village carpenter made it and I painted it for the owner of the toy shop," the signwriter said proudly.

"Did you copy a real horse? It's just like a real horse I've seen," said Rubin.

"There was a horse hobbled[1] on the green opposite, which inspired[2] me to paint the rocking horse in this way," said the signwriter.

"Did you see where it went to?" asked Rubin eagerly.

"No, but just three days ago I saw a dark stranger lead it down the hill yonder," said the signwriter, pointing beyond the village.

Rubin had to decide, whether to leave the signwriter and go in the direction of the horse and stranger or whether to stay for the painting lesson, which the signwriter had so kindly offered to give him?

As there was no certainty that this was the same horse, he chose to stay with the signwriter.

"This large board," said the signwriter, "will become a sign for a new shop, but before I can decorate it with a design and lettering, it will require priming[3] to provide a good surface for me to work on."

The signwriter showed Rubin how to prepare and prime the board by brushing the paint firstly across the grain and then in the same direction as the grain so that an even coat would be applied without any unsightly runs.

Rubin was quick to learn the technique and the signwriter was so pleased that he promised to pay Rubin for his help.

At lunchtime, the signwriter was happy to share some bread from his lunch box and together they crossed the street to drink water from a little stream at the edge of the green and what do you think Rubin found there?-

-Yes, a third golden horseshoe, which, as before, he quickly picked up and tucked into his shirt, so that the signwriter would not notice it.

Then Rubin thought, "This can't have been from the same lost horse, as it has six lines filed on its edge."

He had expected to see one or even four lines. So he went happily back to work with the signwriter.

But in the afternoon, when Rubin had been painting for some time, his mind drifted back to the horse and the latest horseshoe.

"Perhaps this horseshoe does belong to the Grand Duke's horse," he thought, "because no horse has six legs."

Then it seemed more likely to him that the dark stranger had stolen the horse after all.
He was about to pluck up courage to beg leave of the signwriter so that he could proceed with his quest to find the horse, when the signwriter announced that he had got the dame to agree to teach Rubin his letters and numbers and a little math-e-magics in exchange for painting some doors and windows in the classrooms.

Rubin didn't want to let the kind signwriter down, so he agreed to go to the school to paint and to learn all he could with the dame's guidance.

Meanings of some words in chapter two

[1]Hobbled ---- *restrained from wandering**

**The gypsies commonly prevent their horses from straying by tying the two forelegs together.*

[2]Inspired ---- *gave an idea leading to do something.*

[3]Priming ---- *undercoat/s of paint for preserving and sealing wood prior to finishing coats.*

Rubin edged past the horses and saw the farrier amid a shower of fascinating sparks, fashioning a horseshoe that he had just withdrawn from the white-hot coals in the forge.

Chapter III

The farrier, the dame and the tailor

The following day Rubin set out for the school armed with paint and brushes that the signwriter had provided in a cloth bag with a strong leather shoulder strap. On his way he had to pass a forge[1] where there were several horses waiting to be shod by the farrier[2] but the beautiful odd-coloured mare was not among them.

Rubin edged past the horses and saw the farrier among a shower of fascinating sparks, fashioning a horseshoe that he had just withdrawn from the white-hot coals in the forge.

As the farrier paused, at his anvil[3] to wipe his brow, Rubin asked him what the marks meant that he had seen on the golden horseshoes.

"An' where d'ya see those 'orseshoes?" asked the farrier in a quizzical[4] tone.

Rubin pressed an arm tightly to his chest to ensure that the three golden horseshoes were better concealed within his shirt.

"I s-saw them on a horse in the forest," he stammered, which was, I suppose, partly true.

"An' be ye sure they was gold?" asked the farrier in the same tone.

"They were the same colour as the weathercock on the steeple, sir," said Rubin.

"I made tha' tweathercock," said the farrier proudly, "an' I cast the golden bells tha' tang in the tower and made the 'orseshoes too, all from pure gold supplied by the very rich Grand Duke of Merrithorpe. The shoes were for 'is most prized 'orse and while I be busy making them at me anvil, I made the marks you saw.
I al'a's puts different lucky marks on every set of 'orseshoes I makes, 'cos it protects both 'orse and rider."

He paused to think for a moment, then added, “Funny thing is, I don’t know the meaning of those marks me’self, ’cos me ’and is guided in this work by fate. Wat I do know though is tha’ t’oever finds the meaning using ’orse sense[5] will receive good luck and protection.”

“Well,” said Rubin, “the meaning has clearly not been found, because the horse is now missing from the Duke’s stable and I am beginning to suspect that it was stolen back by the dark stranger who is probably the horse-coper who sold the horse in the first place. He is obviously hoping to sell her over and over again.”

“Then we must ’ope,” said the farrier “that ’e brings the ’orse back to me for new shoes and I’ll alert all me farrier mates to look out for ’im too.”

“That won’t be too long,” thought Rubin as he left the forge. “She has already lost three of her shoes” and he clung tightly to all three horseshoes hidden inside his ragged shirt until he was able to transfer them to the bag that the signwriter had provided for him.

Although he had stopped at the forge, Rubin reached the school earlier than the six children who regularly attended, because he was keen and had set out with so much time to spare.

He knocked on the painted front door using the wrought iron knocker - which, incidentally, had been fashioned by the smith, in the form of a horse’s head, and was fixed at a height that the smallest child could easily reach - the dame came to the door to let him in.

“You must be Rubin,” she said, adding, “I spoke only yesterday to the signwriter, so I was expecting you. He told me that you are already an excellent painter and will be able to repair all my chipped paintwork.”

“Yes, I would be pleased to help you Ma’am,” he replied politely.

“I also spoke recently to my friend, the wise woman of the wood,” said the dame, “and she thinks that you may be the young person who promised to help search for the Grand Duke’s lost horse.”

“Yes that was me,” said Rubin, “but I am not having much success.”

“In every endeavour,” said the dame, “you must be patient and then you are most likely to achieve your goals in life. When you have done a little painting for me, I will help you to improve your knowledge and that may well help you to find the lost horse.”

"I believe it was stolen," said Rubin, explaining that the signwriter had seen it led away from the green.

"Well, I hope that the culprit[6] is found," said the dame. Then she showed Rubin the damaged paintwork and left him to do his work.

Rubin was already busy when the six other pupils arrived and, despite the contrast between their clothes and Rubin's dishevelled appearance, they proved to be much more unruly in their behaviour.

One bully took delight in ridiculing Rubin's tattered clothes and failing to get any reaction from the taunting, he decided to kick over the pot of paint, which Rubin was using.

The wise dame, blessed like the crone with a sixth sense, was aware of what had happened and insisted that the bully should first clear up the mess and then find the signwriter, in order to have the paint pot refilled.

By now the signwriter had moved to do work in the next village, so the bully had to walk two miles in each direction.

In those days, paint had to be prepared and thoroughly mixed by hand, so the signwriter was not very pleased when the bully asked for more.

While the bully was away collecting fresh paint, the dame took Rubin to the tailor's shop just across the street, where he was measured for a new suit to replace his tattered and paint spattered clothes.

She had suggested to the tailor that instead of her paying money for the suit, there would be no need for him to pay his daughter's school fees for the following year. An arrangement he was only too pleased to accept.

The tailor was a wizard with needle and thread and Rubin was newly attired and was waiting back at the school before the bully had returned with fresh paint.

The kindly tailor had even provided suitable protective clothing so that Rubin could avoid spoiling his new suit while painting.

------the dame took Rubin to the tailor's shop just across the street, where he was measured for a new suit to replace his tattered and paint-spattered clothes.

After the children had finished school and Rubin had cleaned his paintbrushes, the dame decided to teach him the alphabet.

As Rubin was no longer a child, she was able to explain that the alphabet consisted of twenty-one letters called consonants and five called vowels. The consonants were like the bones in a body and the vowels were like the flesh. Words were generally made up of both. Even though Rubin had soon finished his paintwork in the school and was back working with the signwriter, he continued to have lessons from the dame for several days after normal school hours and he quickly mastered his alphabet and started to learn to spell many useful words.

The signwriter was soon able to let Rubin try his hand at signwriting and was very pleased at how quickly he took to the skill.

The last things that the dame taught Rubin, were his numbers, 1234567890 in that order, together with a little of what she called math-er-magics.

Those ten numbers were of course easy for Rubin to learn, but how they are used, took him a little longer as it does all of us. But because she was such a good teacher, the dame applied magic to the knowledge. Math-er-magics were mathematics made easy.

At the end of one lesson, Rubin felt he could tell the kindly dame more about the runaway horse. He mentioned how when he had seen it in the wood it had seemed to be trying to convey some message by prancing and pirouetting in front of him. He also told her that the wise woman of the wood said it needed to hear its owner speak its name or it would gallop away. Unfortunately, the Grand Duke who had bought the horse from the horse-coper, had been unable to discover its name.

“I have another wise friend,” said the dame, “she is a clairvoyant[7] or fortune-teller and she is especially good at solving such mysteries. I’m sure that if you tell her these things, her help will lead you to discover the horse’s name and perhaps to recovering her for the Grand Duke.”

The dame then explained where the clairvoyant lived in a caravan on the moor, about a mile away.

Meanings of some words in chapter three

[1]Forge ---- *a blacksmith's workplace also his hearth for heating metal.*

[2]Farrier ---- *a smith who shoes horses.*

[3]Anvil ---- *a heavy block of iron on which the smith shapes his metalwork by hammering.*

[4]Quizzical ---- *puzzled.*

[5]Horse sense ---- *commonsense.*

[6]Culprit ---- *a person responsible for a crime or misdeed.*

[7]Clairvoyant ---- *a person with the ability to see beyond that of normal senses.*

Chapter IV

The clairvoyant

The very next weekend Rubin set out to cross the moor.

In a little clearing between some bushes on the far side he saw a group of five gypsy caravans. There were several horses tethered or hobbled nearby, but none was as beautiful as the mare he was searching for.

When he got to the first caravan, he asked a young girl, who was busy feeding her chickens, where the wise woman of the moor lived and she directed him to the furthest of the five, where a woman, clad in a brightly coloured shawl, was sitting on the steps leading to the caravan door.

Rubin noticed that the caravan was much in need of painting and, that much of the gold leaf scrollwork was flaking away.

“Are you the wise woman of the moor?” Rubin asked the woman.

“I am indeed, my dear bless-ed,” said the clairvoyant, “and because of my sixth sense, I have been expecting you, so come in, come in, my dear.”

Rubin entered shyly and, once inside the caravan, he noticed some of the paraphernalia[1] that goes with being a gypsy clairvoyant and fortune-teller.

A large crystal ball stood on a little table,

A kettle boiled on the little black stove for making tea and two teacups stood upside-down on their saucers.

There were other things Rubin didn’t recognise, like playing cards with grotesque[2] figures on them.

“What do you wish for, my dear bless-ed?” said the clairvoyant.

“I wi—I,” stammered Rubin.

Was it too late? He realised he had almost started his third wish.

"Are you the Wise Woman of the Moor?" Rubin asked the woman.

"Come on, dearie, don't be shy," said the clairvoyant.

Rubin changed his approach. "The dame from the school suggested that you might be able to help me solve a riddle," he said, "so that I can find a missing horse."

"Tell me the riddle, then," said the clairvoyant.

"That's the big problem," said Rubin. "It's not a human sort of riddle, it's a riddle that I think the horse was trying to tell me as she was running away."

With that, Rubin told his entire story, especially explaining how the horse had nodded and pranced and pirouetted in front of him, but he left out any bits about the three golden horseshoes, which were still safely hidden inside the bag slung over his shoulder.

"To solve that," said the clairvoyant, "will call for my utmost concentration, because I will have to translate the horse language into human words."

"Can you really do that?" asked Rubin.

"Oh yes," she replied, then added, "But it is also usual dearie, for my clients to cross my palm with silver, especially to pay for such an effort as this."

"I don't have any silver," said Rubin, clutching the bag containing the gold horseshoes tightly to his side.

"Perhaps, my bless-ed, as you are learning to be a signwriter, you would re-paint my caravan instead of giving me money."

The kindly Rubin quickly agreed to come again the following weekend, to start painting the caravan.

The clairvoyant seemed to go into a trance, then after much cogitating[3], incantations[4] and unmelodious[5] ranting[6] about three wise women, three horseshoes, and three nearly used up wishes, she concluded that the problem could be solved by using the magic number three. Then, she took a quill pen from behind her right ear and wrote the following verses upon a scrap of parchment.

THE HORSE'S RIDDLE

Ask three friends for different lucky numbers (nought to nine),

Write the three together closely and inline,

Reverse the group of three and write them down again,

Two sets of three made clear and bold and plain.

The smaller from the larger group now take,

And next reverse the answer that you make,

Add these two rows and multiply by three,

The number that you get is now the key,

Its secret you must keep within your mind,

My name, with horse sense you may later find,

With all the numbers which the Dame has taught,

From one, in order finishing with nought.

“That, my dear bless-ed,” said the clairvoyant, “is, for the time being at least, all I can do for you. You must now go back to the dame, because with her help and that of some of the children at her school, you should be able to solve the riddle and find the name of the horse quite easily.”

Rubin was so pleased, that he skipped from the caravan all the way across the moor and back to the signwriter's workshop where he was now staying. He then lay down on some sacks and slept soundly.

Dear reader, while Rubin sleeps, can you solve the horses riddle?

After he awoke the next morning he set off eagerly for the dame's school.

Meanings of some words in chapter four

[1]Paraphernalia ---- *items for a particular activity.*
[2]Grotesque ---- *ugly.*
[3]Cogitating ---- *considering.*
[4]Incantations ---- *words associated with a magic spell.*
[5]Unmelodious ---- *not tuneful.*
[6]Ranting ---- *wild yelling.*

Chapter V

The Grand Duke's castle

At the Dame's School the next day Rubin explained how the clairvoyant had translated[1] the horse's riddle from horse language into English and that she had suggested that the dame and her pupils might like to help him solve it. *Hopefully, dear readers, you have already solved it but, just in case, this is what happened next:*

He showed the written verses of the riddle and the dame gathered together her class of children, asking three of them to provide the different numbers, which she wrote on the blackboard.

Then she reversed their order and subtracted the smaller line of three from the larger, reversed the answer and added, just as the riddle said, and got the boy who had been the bully and was now much nicer, to multiply by three.

Rubin was very surprised at the answer (3267) and felt he had probably discovered the number of marks that he might have seen on the fourth horseshoe if he had found it. Because, if you remember, the first horseshoe that he had found had three marks, the second had two and the third six.

After that, the dame wrote the words HORSE SENSE, in big bold capital letters on her black board and she asked Rubin to number the letters, in the order he had been taught.

H	O	R	S	E	S	E	N	S	E
1	2	3	4	5	6	7	8	9	0

"Now, Rubin," she said, "You can solve the name of the horse by using only the letters over the numbers 3,2,6 and 7."

Of course Rubin was very pleased when he realised it was ROSE

The next weekend Rubin went back across the moor, armed with everything he needed to paint the caravan belonging to the wise clairvoyant woman.

As soon as he arrived, she asked him if he had managed to solve the riddle and he was able to say how pleased he was that he had.

To restore the caravan paintwork took many weekends so Rubin had to return again and again but he had good reason not to mind. On each occasion he went, he saw the girl who had first shown him where the clairvoyant lived. She was usually outside scattering corn around her caravan to feed her chickens and it seemed to Rubin that she was becoming more and more beautiful every time he saw her.

In order to see the girl more often, he asked the clairvoyant if he might repaint the board, which advertised her fortune telling.

Each time he crossed the moor; he looked out for Rose the missing horse as well as the girl.
He always caught sight of the girl, but there was no sign of Rose.

On one occasion there were many more horses gathered near the caravans because there was a horse fair.
Rubin examined all of the horses that had been taken there for trading, by a horse-coper, but there was no sign of Rose and no sound reason to accuse the man of stealing her.

His weekday work with the signwriter took Rubin to many different places. The most interesting of these was the castle belonging to the Grand Duke where many colourful heraldic[2] panels had to be repainted in dazzling colours and gold leaf.

Rubin became such a proficient[3] apprentice that he was often entrusted to work alone.

One day while he was busy in the castle, the Grand Duke came into the Great Hall to compliment Rubin on his work.

"Young man," said the Duke, "this is really incredible workmanship for someone so young."

"Thank you, sir," said Rubin politely and, because the Duke seemed to be a kind man, he felt confident enough to say, "I've been trying to

"Young man," said the Duke, "this is really incredible workmanship for someone so young."

find your missing horse, sir, without success, but I have been able to discover that her name is Rose."

"How did you manage that?" asked the Duke.

Rubin had to tell the whole story, but he did not mention the three golden horseshoes he had found, not because he was dishonest, but because he thought it would be nice to return them together with Rose, the horse.

"I intend to find her and bring her back to you, sir," said Rubin.

"I will be pleased to spare you enough time from your work here inside my castle if you use that time to look for her," replied the Duke and he added, "I will give a great reward to whoever brings her safely back to me."

Mindful of this added incentive[4], Rubin headed through the forest beyond the castle gates and towards the village after his day's work.

The forest was clad in snow and, as he passed through it, he heard several unfamiliar noises, but he was particularly startled by a dragging sound close by.

"Hello again, young man," said a quavering voice from the darkness. It was the crone and she was dragging a huge bundle of dry sticks, all tied together.

"May I help you with those?" asked Rubin.

"Yes please," she said.

Rubin followed her to her hut, adding more sticks to the bundle on the way there.

"These will keep you warm for much of the winter," said Rubin.

Together they sat by the fire in her little hut, while the crone brewed tea and she told Rubin that she had again seen the horse, this time being led across the boundary of the Grand Duke's estate to the Land-of-Un far beyond.

"I have been helped by the dame and the clairvoyant to find the horse's name," said Rubin, "and I will go to the Land-of-Un to search for her and to bring her back to the Duke."

"Then you must be very careful," said the crone, "for the people that live there are **un**canny, **un**godly, **un**welcoming, **un**pleasant, **un**trustworthy, **un**couth, **un**tidy, **un**caring, **un**bearable and many more **uns** which I can't think of for the moment.
There is only one way in and out of the land and you will have to search several miles of its perimeter to gain access. The thorn bushes are poisonous and you must not eat any of the berries or fruit of that land for it is all **un**palatable and cursed."

Rubin thanked the crone for her advice and hospitality[5], and made his way home to the signwriter's workshop.

Meanings of some words in chapter five

[1]Translated ---- *words expressed in another language.*

[2]Heraldic ---- *relating to symbols used on coats of arms and armorial bearings.*

[3]Proficient ---- *skilled.*

[4]Incentive ---- *something promised or given to encourage.*

[5]Hospitality ---- *friendliness and generosity*

Chapter VI

Rubin's ordeal in the Land-of-Un

Before venturing into the Land-of-Un, Rubin was sensible enough to inform all of his friends that he was going to be away for a long while, probably many years. He told the farrier and the clairvoyant, He told the dame and the school children. Of course, he told the signwriter, who, because it was winter, was now painting Christmas toys in the shelter of the toyshop.

"I've nearly finished these toys," said the signwriter, "so I will be more than happy to continue the work in the castle while you're away, then the Duke will not have to wait until you return and I will tell him you have gone to the Land-of-Un, to look for his horse."

Because Rubin had been earning money for his work, he had bought himself some strong boots from the village cobbler[1], and a warm sheepskin topcoat, from the furrier[2], together with gloves and a fur hat which had ear flaps. So he was well equipped for his adventure.

He set off early in the morning, making his way through the forest, which provided much protection from the snow, already lying quite thickly upon the ground.
After a little while, Rubin smelled the pleasant smell of wood smoke drifting towards him and he knew he was near to the crone's hut once again.
Suddenly and noiselessly, the crone appeared before him and she pressed something into his hand.

"That is a little talisman[3] to protect you and bring you back safely," said the crone, then she added, "you have many miles to travel and you will be away for a long time possibly some years and you will need all the good luck my simple gift will provide".

Then she waved him goodbye and disappeared just as suddenly and noiselessly into the darkness of the snow-laden trees.

As Rubin hung the talisman by its string around his neck he saw it was a pearlescent[4] shell.
It took Rubin several months before he reached the impenetrable[5] thorn bushes that prevented easy access to The Land-of-Un.
It was rumoured that this natural hedge was half a mile wide and that its thorns were extremely poisonous, but none of Rubin's friends really knew, as they had not ventured into that land themselves.

Rubin walked for miles along the boundary, occasionally venturing into gaps which he thought might lead to open land on the other side, but always the gap came to a dead end and he had to go back outside the boundary and try again.

He managed to find a few mushrooms by scraping away snow from the ground and this had supplemented[6] the parcel of food he had taken with him.

He walked on and on for many weeks and began to feel that he had completely explored the perimeter[7] of the land when he found another gap much narrower than most and which he would have missed, had it not been for seeing the footprints made by a wily fox which must have entered the Duke's vast estate in search of an unsuspecting rabbit.

After walking through the gap for what seemed an eternity, Rubin found himself in the mysterious Land-of-Un.
Where the snow had been blown clear by an icy wind, the slightly undulating[8] landscape appeared to be barren, only a few trees survived, mainly stunted and twisted forebears of the thorns which Rubin had struggled to pass.

The area was vast and a dark hollow at its centre seemed to indicate to Rubin that he was on a huge flat and almost circular plateau[9].

It seemed to take Rubin forever to reach the centre and there, as he suspected, was a deep shaded valley, the almost vertical sides of which he knew he would not be able to climb down.

Through the shade and some rising mist, he could just make out one village below in the middle of fields covered in snow.

He walked around the rim of the valley until he found less steep slopes, but they too were covered in slippery layers of snow and ice.

He chose the least steep descent, the only one he could risk, but once started, he could not stop and he slipped and slithered without control most of the way down.
At the bottom he could see the distant houses, which he approached stealthily, from the shaded side of the valley.

Perhaps he was in luck, because he could see a large paddock between some stone cottages and there were a great number of horses pawing at the snow in order to graze there.
The paddock was unfenced for there was no easy escape from the village, which was hemmed in by the surrounding steep escarpment[10].

Dusk, was already starting to fall over the scene.
Probably because of the bitter cold, nobody was to be seen outside and so Rubin felt it would be safe to move a little closer.
He was in luck, for in the midst of several piebald, skewbald, chestnut, bay and grey horses, was one extremely beautiful odd-coloured horse.

He got closer and closer. "Rose," he whispered, but the horse could not hear him through the long mane, which had blown up and covered the ear which faced him.
"Rose," he said again in a louder tone, but she still did not hear.
The other horses looked uncomfortable they had seen Rubin in his furs and believed him to be a wolf or some other predatory[11] animal.

All, except Rose, fled to the opposite side of the paddock, whinnying and snorting with fear, but the braver Rose turned to face the threat.

"Rose, it's me!" yelled Rubin and he removed his hat to show more of his face.

Rose moved towards him, a little unsure at first, so to tempt her closer Rubin held out an apple, the last of his food. But there was no need. Rose suddenly broke into a trot, having recognised his face.

She gently thrust her warm muzzle into Rubin's shoulder; meanwhile, the other horses were still creating a disturbance by whinnying at the other side of the field.

"You must come with me, my beauty," said Rubin. "There's no time to waste, so come on Rose, kinder people in Merrithorpe will look after you better than this. I'm going to take you away from here, so follow me, come on, we must move quickly."

As Rubin walked away, Rose followed responding well to his gentle persuasion.
Just then a light appeared at the nearest doorway. It was a man with a lantern. The whinnying of the other horses had alerted him.
Rose reared up at the sight of him.

"Hey, you!" shouted the man.

Thinking it was the horse-coper he had seen at the horse fair on the moor, Rubin hesitated to make sure, but Rose had already bolted away from the scene.

By following the marks of her hooves in the snow and running as fast as he could, Rubin eventually caught up with the horse at the base of the slope he had previously slid down.

He looked back and now there were several angry men brandishing clubs and various improvised weapons.

"We have to go up there, Rose," said Rubin and he made a start up the lower slope, coaxing Rose as he climbed.

Although night was closing in, a full moon lit up the snow and aided their vision.
Climbing higher, Rubin realized that he had dragged much of the snow from the rocky slope which he had slid down and, by picking his way carefully he was able to make slow progress, with Rose following closely behind.

The men in pursuit were now closing in on them, yelling threats and making menacing gestures.
Soon the men were a quarter of the way up the winding hazardous route that Rubin and Rose were taking and they were not many yards behind.

Rose was above an overhang of rock which seemed to have gathered more snow. Rubin feared she might slip, especially when she kicked-out towards the men below.

In so doing she disturbed a great volume of snow, which gathered more in its path forming a small avalanche[12] which engulfed[13] most of the men and swept others to the valley floor.
But one man, the horse-coper, had diverted[14] to another route, one that he was familiar with and his progress was more rapid than that of Rubin and Rose. He reached the top first, by which time day was beginning to break making it easy for him to find his way along the edge of the plateau to the point where he expected Rubin and Rose to appear.

Rose made her final scramble and appeared at the top of the escarpment less than a yard from the man.

Then, standing in the horse's path, the horse-coper spread his arms wide, holding a coiled rope in one hand and still brandishing a wooden club in the other.

The horse's greatest fear was of certain death if she fell from the precipice[15]. She reared up on her hind legs, then with head down and neck arched, she charged straight at her adversary[16].
Although the man was used to horse behaviour, she had taken him by surprise and he failed to throw the rope over her neck. Dropping the club from his other hand, he made a desperate grab for her long flowing mane.

Now completely incensed[17], she galloped, dragging him through the snow across the plateau.

When Rubin finally reached the top, he could only see at a considerable distance a cloud of snow, scattered by horse and man. Eventually the horse-coper let go of Rose's mane, having been cut and bruised by the rocks beneath the snow.

The horse disappeared from Rubin's sight but in the early dawn light, he could just make out the man lying motionless in the path Rose had made in the snow.
Rubin picked up the club, which had been dropped and followed.
On reaching the man, he saw it was definitely the same person he had seen at the horse fair on the moor.

Then, standing in the horse's path, the horse-coper spread his arms wide, holding a coiled rope in one hand and brandishing a wooden club in the other.

Surprisingly, the man was only winded, he started to get to his feet, but when Rubin brandished the heavy club over his head he hesitated.

"Why are you trying to steal my horse?" asked the horse-coper.

"You are the thief," said Rubin. "I know she is not your horse. You stole her from the Grand Duke of Merrithorpe, who you once sold her to and I believe you stole her in order to sell her over and over again. I intend to take her back to the Duke."

"And do you think you will succeed?" said the man, who could now see some men who had survived the avalanche, approaching Rubin from behind.

Stupidly, as they got closer they broke into a tumult of angry shouting which alerted Rubin to their presence, so he ran on in the direction Rose had taken.
Being young and healthy, Rubin was able to put a good distance between himself and the men, but the chase continued for many days until Rubin reached the thorns which formed the boundary around the Land-of-Un.

Although he tried and tried, he could not find the path through the thorns.
Very soon, two men had caught up and he had to run right and left, left and right to dodge them. He was tiring fast.
Suddenly, Rose appeared from a gap in the hedge where she had been hiding. She ran round and round Rubin, kicking outward toward the men as a mare would if protecting a foal.
For a second, she stopped with a flank presented to Rubin and recognizing the invitation, he leapt onto her back.

Rose quickly turned, scattering the men and gathering momentum drove herself deep into the thorn bushes, with Rubin hanging tightly onto her mane.
The poisonous thorns tore deep into her hide, tearing her flesh, but she rushed on. The thorns pierced Rubin's legs too, even his thick boots provided little protection, but Rose thrust herself on and on through that vast thickness of thorn hedge until they emerged back in the Duke's forest.

It was then that poor Rose collapsed to the ground, both with the effects of the poisonous thorns and from total exhaustion from her efforts.

Rubin listened to see if the men were daring to follow, but there was no sound; clearly they had given up the chase.

He then knelt beside Rose and soothed and stroked her trembling body, washing away blood from her wounded flanks with the cooling snow. Then, laying his talisman on her side, he whispered, “I’m going to get help.”

Meanings of some words in chapter six

[1]Cobbler ---- *a shoemaker.*
[2]Furrier ---- *a fur trader.*
[3]Talisman ---- *a lucky charm.*
[4]Pearlescent ---- *having the lustre of pearl.*
[5]Impenetrable ---- *impossible to pass through.*
[6]Supplemented ---- *added to.*
[7]Perimeter ---- *boundary around an area.*
[8]Undulating ---- *having a wavy form.*
[9]Plateau ---- *an area of high and fairly level ground.*
[10]Escarpment ---- *a long steep slope at the edge of a plateau.*
[11]Predatory ---- *an animal that preys on others.*
[12]Avalanche ---- *a rapidly falling mass of snow and ice.*
[13]Engulfed ---- *covered over.*
[14]Diverted ---- *changed course.*
[15]Precipice ---- *a steep rock face or cliff.*
[16]Adversary ---- *an opponent.*
[17]Incensed ---- *made angry.*

Chapter VII

The clairvoyant's cure

It was some time before Rubin began to notice the sweet smell of wood smoke, but long before he reached the hut he saw a light coming towards him. It was the crone, now looking very old; she had not slept well for a long time and her sixth sense had told her something was not right.

With the aid of her gnarled stick she accompanied Rubin back to where Rose still lay motionless at the foot of the poisonous thorn hedge.

Rubin managed to start a small fire, with the flint and dry material he always carried, while the crone searched beneath the trees for a few leaves of plants that she knew would provide an antidote[1] for the poison. Unfortunately very few of these leaves had survived the recent frost, so she was unable to concoct[2] sufficient of the healing potion. In fact so small was the quantity of leaves that Rubin's little shell talisman served as a tiny cauldron[3] for the brew and a cup to drink it from.

Despite his own wounds, Rubin insisted that all of the antidote should be used to heal the brave horse, but there wasn't even enough, for that purpose alone.

In the morning Rose had recovered a little, but Rubin could no longer stand.
With the crone's help, he just managed to get onto the horse's back and with her gentle encouragement they all made it to the warmth and shelter of her hut.

Although they rested there for several days, Rubin's sickness continued to get worse and Rose, probably from her efforts in carrying Rubin to the hut, suffered a complete relapse[4]. They both had high fevers and drifted in and out of consciousness[5].

Fearing they would both die, the crone decided that she had to make, what for her would be, a superhuman effort in order to help them both.

With the aid of her gnarled stick, she accompanied Rubin back to where Rose still lay motionless at the foot of the poisonous thorn hedge.

She had heard that the clairvoyant could use the magical power of words alone, to cure many of the gypsies' ills.

Leaning heavily on her stick, the old crone managed to get as far as the village and luckily, there on the green opposite the toyshop, she found the clairvoyant's caravan with all the others. They had decided to move away from the area and were just obtaining a few provisions for their journey.

Having listened to the crone's story, the clairvoyant lapsed yet again into a trance, accompanied by much cogitating, incantations, and similar unmelodious rantings.

When she regained her composure, she took her quill pen from behind her ear and wrote upon a scrap of parchment a simple verse.

Then, she handed the verse to the crone, saying, "This is all I can do for now, my dear bless-ed. For the cure to work you must solve this simple riddle."

THE CLAIRVOYANT'S CURE

This sickness, is your work old Devil,
Contrived with poisonous thorns,
Now turn around this act of EVIL,
Before tomorrow dawns.

Can you solve the riddle to cure Rose and Rubin?

Well, it did not take the crone too long to realise that if she turned around EVIL before dawn, both Rubin and Rose would be cured.
So as fast as her old legs (and the walking stick) would allow, she hurried back towards her hut and as soon as she was within earshot of Rubin and Rose she started to yell "LIVE," she yelled it over and over again "LIVE, LIVE, LIVE."

Would you believe it, by the following morning, the fever had left them, they were both well again and even the wounds caused by the thorn bushes were completely healed!

Rubin expressed his joy for all that the crone and the clairvoyant had done in nursing Rose and himself back to health.
To thank the crone, he collected a huge pile of firewood, which he stored beneath the overhanging eaves of her hut, more than enough to last another winter.

"Now that she is well, I must take Rose back to the Duke," he told the crone.

Rubin said goodbye promising to let her know later how pleased the Duke was.

"You must keep this with you," said the crone, again handing him the talisman.

With that, Rubin walked away from the hut, with Rose following closely behind.

Meanings of some words in chapter seven

[1]Antidote ---- *medicine to counteract a poison.*

[2]Concoct ---- *create with ingredients.*

[3]Cauldron ---- *a cooking pot used on an open fire.*

[4]Relapse ---- *deterioration in health after signs of improvement.*

[5]Consciousness ---- *the minds awareness of being alive.*

Chapter VIII

The Duke gets his horse back

ubin crossed the drawbridge into the castle, with Rose still behind him. He was met in the courtyard by the short-sighted butler who, not seeing Rose at first, said:

"And I suppose you'll be back to do more painting?"

"Yes, sir, if the Duke will still have me," answered Rubin, "but first, I have to give him his horse."

"I will go and find the Duke then," said the butler and he disappeared into the castle, slamming a heavy door behind him.

Before the Duke appeared, Rubin had found a rope and tied Rose with a very secure knot to a ring in the wall beside the door.

He wrapped both of his arms about her neck and whispered in her ear that all would be well.

Then, because he did not wish to appear as if he were waiting for a reward, he walked away from the castle across the drawbridge back to the village and the sign writer's workshop.

At first, the Duke was thrilled to find Rose.
He examined her thoroughly, frequently speaking her name, so that she was quite happy with him.
He could see that she was in good condition, but he soon noticed that she no longer had her golden horseshoes.
Some suspicious[1] thoughts crept into his mind.

"Was the young man that the butler had seen really Rubin, the signwriter's apprentice? If so, why had he not waited?"

Then he wondered if Rubin had been the horse thief all along.

The next thing the Duke did was to put a saddle on Rose and he walked her to the farrier asking him to fit new shoes.

He wrapped both of his arms about her neck and whispered in her ear that all would be well.

“Ah,” said the farrier, “I thawt she would not keep they pure gold shoes on ’er feet for too long, sir, they be not really suitable.
They nails ’ave almost certainly pulled right through, because pure gold be a very soft metal, it be, sir” He added, “ ’oever finds they gold shoes sir, will be rich, indeed ’e will, sir.”

The Duke snorted and said. “Then my good man, you had better fit iron shoes this time.”

While the farrier was shaping the set of new shoes for Rose, the Duke asked if he had seen Rubin, the signwriter’s apprentice.

“Why yes, sir, ’e’s jus’ returned me sign, ’e ’as. Dun a good job, ’e did, doan’ it look good, sir?”

“I need to see him,” said the Duke grumpily

“Well, sir,” I’m sure e’ll be back busy in ’is workshop, ’e will, sir.”

The Duke riding the newly shod[2] Rose, set off across the green, in the direction of the signwriter’s workshop.
Rubin was busy inside but the signwriter met the Duke at the door.

“Where’s that apprentice of yours?” asked the Duke.

“He’s inside, sir,” said the signwriter, “and we’re all so pleased he brought your horse back to you.”

“Is that what he told you?” asked the still suspicious Duke.

“Oh! No, sir, he’s not the sort to brag,” said the signwriter, “but many people in the village have learned that the crone with the aid of the clairvoyant’s cure had managed to revive both the horse and Rubin, because they were both so ill after their terrifying ordeal in the Land-of-Un.”

“And where is the clairvoyant now?” asked the Duke.

“She went north with the rest of the caravans,” said the signwriter.

The Duke was now quite satisfied that Rubin was innocent[3].

“I’d like to see the young man, I owe him my gratitude[4],” he said.

Rubin was called to the door and the Duke thanked him over and over again. Then he promised that if Rubin would be patient for a while, he would provide a very special reward.

“Thank you, sir,” said Rubin and he gave Rose an affectionate[5] pat before the Duke rode back to his castle.

Meanings of some words in chapter eight

[1]*Suspicious* ---- *distrustful.*

[2]*Shod* ---- *fitted with shoes.*

[3]*Innocent* ---- *not guilty of an offence.*

[4]*Gratitude* ---- *thankfulness.*

[5]*Affectionate* ---- *showing fondness.*

Chapter IX

A riddle about a girl

he gypsies with their five caravans headed on their migration[1] back to the south and halted on the village green in time for the Michaelmas[2] celebrations.

The clairvoyant set up her board outside of her caravan, its message, which Rubin had painted the previous year, stated:

Gypsy Adeline
Clairvoyant Supreme

Fortunes told
Palms read
Tea leaves studied

Fee one silver sixpence only,
Per fifteen minute consultation.

Rubin joined the excited queue by the board.
On reaching the front, the clairvoyant welcomed him in and he told her how pleased the Duke had been with everyone who helped to have his horse returned safely.

"Well my dearie, here you are before me yet again," said the clairvoyant. "I have helped you twice before and on each occasion I said, 'that is all for the time being,' but this, the third time will be the last and most important of all."

"I will not charge you," she added, "because I still owe you for all the painting which you have done."

"But," interrupted Rubin, "you have since saved my life and that of Rose, the horse."

"That was my special pleasure, my dear bless-ed," said the clairvoyant. Then she stared into her crystal ball once more, with of course, the trance, the cogitating, the incantations, and the unmelodious rantings.

When she had recovered her composure she said, "I have seen a beautiful girl and she is looking at something shining brightly upon the ground, it is the sign of her destiny and yours, a golden horseshoe with seven marks upon its edge. You must find her, my dearie."

"How do I do that?" asked Rubin.

Once more, she took the quill pen from behind her right ear and wrote the following verse upon a scrap of parchment, which she handed to Rubin.

THE CLAIRVOYANT'S FINAL RIDDLE

Turn round four special numbers, which solved the horse's name,
Divide them all by seven, please complete this game,
With horse sense as before, you'll surely find a clue,
That leads you to a special girl, the one who waits for you.

"Good luck with this my last riddle, my dear bless-ed," said the clairvoyant, as Rubin left her caravan.

Can you solve the clairvoyant's last riddle before Rubin gets back to the signwriter's workshop?

Did you, like Rubin, manage to solve it?

When later that day, Rubin arrived back at the signwriter's workshop, he studied the final riddle and he quickly realised that the dame had imparted enough knowledge and horse sense for him to solve it. So he wrote firstly the four numbers that had solved the horse's name.

3267

Then he turned them round

7623

Then he divided by seven

1089

And numbering H O R S E S E N S E
1 2 3 4 5 6 7 8 9 0

The letters over 1089 gave him the clue HENS

"Of course," said Rubin to himself, "HENS! HENS! The girl I always see on the moor when I visit the clairvoyant, she keeps hens."

He knew he had to set out across the moor, to where the gypsies had again made their camp, and he did so early the next day.

As he approached the first caravan he noticed the girl scattering corn onto the ground from a trug[3] that she was carrying. Several chicken were pecking at the ground around her.
Then, still at some distance, he saw her stoop and take something from the ground placing it in the trug.

He felt a little nervous, but just as he was getting nearer, one of the hens for some strange reason panicked and ran towards him. Rubin tried to stop it, but it changed direction and rushed back towards the girl.

In complete confusion the hen then dashed madly to and fro between them as they closed in on it.

They both made a grab for it and as they did so, the bag hanging from Rubin's shoulder swung forward spilling its contents,

In complete confusion the hen then dashed madly to and fro between them as they closed in on it.

including the three golden horseshoes, onto the ground between them. At the same time, the girl lost her grip on the handle of the trug from which, the remainder of the corn spilt and what do you think lay glinting in the middle of that patch of spilt corn?

Yes, it was the fourth horseshoe!

Meanwhile the hen had taken to the air and finished up from whence it came with all the other hens. They both laughed and the girl thanked Rubin for his help.

Rubin was puzzled. “Where did you find that horseshoe?” He asked.

“I found it lying in the grass, a moment ago, as I was scattering the corn,” replied the girl and she took it quickly from the ground and hid it behind her back saying, “finders keepers!”

Rubin guessed this was true having seen her pick something up from the ground shortly before.

“My name’s Rubin,” he said, then he asked, “what’s yours?”

Still hiding the horseshoe, the girl ignored his question. “Where did you find the three horseshoes you dropped?” she asked.

Rubin related his past adventures, telling how he had found the three horseshoes, how he had discovered Rose’s name and that he had gone to the Land-of-Un to rescue her from the horse-coper, finally returning her to her rightful owner, the Duke.

“You are very brave,” she said, “but why didn’t you give your three horseshoes back to the Duke?”

“Because,” replied Rubin. “I’d hoped to find the fourth horseshoe and to return them all together.”

The girl then related how a very unpleasant horse-coper had once tried to trade horses with the gypsies but had refused to sell one very beautiful horse.

“I think that must have been Rose, and I think that is when she must have lost this shoe,” she said as she showed the fourth horseshoe to Rubin.

It was clear to Rubin that the horse-coper wanted to get Rose away from the area so that the Duke could not claim her back.

"You still haven't told me your name," Rubin said to the girl.

"You'll have to guess my name, or solve it, just like you did for Rose," she teased.

Rubin tried all the girls' names he knew, which wasn't very many and he found he was just as unsuccessful as the Duke had been in trying to guess Rose's name.

"No, no, no," said the girl in answer to each one, then she added, "my name sits right in the middle of a lucky number."

Rubin still couldn't think what she meant. He tried over and over to find names in the numbers the dame had taught him but did not succeed. "I give up," he said.

"I've told you it's in the middle of a number and the number is on this horseshoe which I'm not showing you until you guess."

"Oh! I understand!" said Rubin. "That horseshoe has seven lines marked on it, S-E-V-E-N and right in the middle of the number seven is your name E-V-E.

"You've got it!" she said, feeling rather pleased for him.

"We have to give all of the horseshoes back to their true owner," said Rubin.

"I would give mine, if I knew how to find the Duke," said Eve.

She agreed when Rubin suggested they should go together to see the Duke with all four horseshoes and the next day they met again and set off for the castle.

On their way, they chatted easily.

"I remember once showing you where the wise woman of the moor lived" said Eve, "and, since then, I've seen you painting her caravan."

Rubin explained how helpful the clairvoyant had been with her riddles, but he didn't dare to tell her yet about the final riddle.

They arrived at the Castle crossing the moat to the courtyard by means of the drawbridge, which had been left down. Then Rubin rang the bell at the side of the huge oak door and after some time the old butler appeared.
At Rubin's request he went to fetch the Duke and the Duke sent the butler back to bring them both into the great hall.

Eve had never seen inside a castle before and she remarked on the wonderful Heraldic shields, which Rubin had repainted.

"This young man is very clever," said the Duke. "He painted most of these shields until he decided to go to the Land-of-Un to find my horse."

"Together," said Rubin looking towards Eve and modestly changing the subject, "together we have found all of the missing horseshoes."

"I am still planning to give you a special reward for recovering my horse," said the Duke to Rubin. "I hope you are still being patient, but in the meantime I suggest you each keep the horseshoes you found because they seem to have brought you both so much good luck."

Then, seeing that Eve and Rubin were quite suited to each other, he added with a twinkle in his eye, "I believe they will certainly add to the good fortune of both of you and that will please me."

Then, with a farewell from the Duke, they left the castle together.

Meanings of some words in chapter nine

[1]Migration ---- *moving to a new area to find work or for improved climate.*

[2]Michaelmas ---- *the feast of St Michael on 29th of September.*

[3]Trug ---- *a shallow basket made of strips of wood.*

Chapter X

Peels of joy

n a sunny day the following spring the old church tower was rocking as the golden bells rang out their dulcet[1] tones and the little golden weather cock clearly shared in the joy by spinning round and round on top of the tall church spire.

The newly wedded Rubin and Eve left the church and walked towards the lychgate[2] past all of their friends.

Each wore one of two gold wedding rings and Eve also wore two large golden earrings. Rubin had arranged for the village jeweller to make all of these from the horseshoe with the two marks.

The remainder of the same horseshoe was taken to a gold beater who hammered the ductile[3] metal, making it into gold sheets each finer than Eve's raven hair.

There were so many of these fine sheets of gold that both Rubin and the signwriter were able to apply gold leaf on Heraldic shields and Caravans and Shop signs and Inn signs for the rest of their lives.

At the lychgate, the newly-weds were covered in rose petals and rice scattered from all sides.

"I feel a bit like one of my hens being thrown their corn," said Eve.

"It's a good job they're not throwing corn," said Rubin, "that might sting even more than the rice."

All their friends wished them well and then the Duke stepped forward from the crowd. He was leading Rose, together with a tiny foal, a miniature version of Rose.

"I noticed that Rose was in foal when I examined her just after Rubin returned her to the castle," said the Duke." Then to the surprise and delight of both Rubin and Eve, he added:

"These two horses are for you; my groom and I are both getting too old to give them as much happiness as you can. So I hope you will all be very happy together."

"These two horses are for you, my groom and myself are getting too old to give them as much happiness as you can. So I hope you will all be very happy together".

They were both overjoyed at such wonderful wedding presents. With his permission, they named the little stallion[4] foal Archibald, after the Grand Duke Sir ARCHIBALD of MERRITHORPE.

The wedding reception was held in a Wayside Inn just outside of the village. It was called. –

Rubin had recently painted the smart new sign, which hung from a fancy bracket over the door and he had applied gold leaf to the four horseshoes portrayed[5] on it.

The Old Crone and the Grand Duke,
The Dame and the Signwriter,
The Clairvoyant and the Farrier,
and all the children from the Dame School, including the completely reformed bully, were invited to the reception.

Rose and Archibald were given extra hay and had a stopover in the stable of the Inn.

Even the <u>seven</u> hens had been treated to an extra <u>seven</u> hands full of corn, because the <u>seven</u> eggs, which they had dutifully laid the night before, were served at the wedding breakfast.
That magic and lucky number <u>seven</u> had come to mean a lot to Eve and Rubin, especially when Rubin pointed out that the numbers on the remaining horseshoes (3, 6 &7) added up to 16 (which was Eve's

age when they first met) and that 1+ 6 also equals 7, which was the number that had brought them together. Those three remaining horseshoes (numbers 3, 6 & 7) were held in safekeeping, sensibly saved for a rainy day.
Rubin and Eve went away the day after their wedding for a springtime honeymoon, travelling in Eve's newly painted caravan pulled by Rose, with Archibald her foal alongside.
A small crowd had gathered to wave them off as they set out from Merrithorpe, clip clop, clip clop.

Nobody in Merrithorpe was ever troubled by the horse-coper again, and they all continued to be one of the merriest communities for ever after.

Finally dear readers, I hope you enjoyed this story. I'm sure you can see the importance of using common sense (horse sense) in your lives. Like Rubin, take advantage of opportunities to learn and improve yourselves and then you will find your whole lives more complete, worthwhile and interesting.

Good luck & best wishes S.W.P

Meanings of some words in chapter ten

[1]Dulcet ---- *sweet and soothing (relating to sound).*

[2]Lychgate ---- *a roofed gateway to a church.*

[3]Ductile ---- *easily worked (relating to bending and shaping metals).*

[4]Stallion ---- *an adult male horse.*

[5]Portrayed ---- *represented or depicted.*